I0557159

Thanks for buying this book, appreciated.

Introducing 'The SODS'

Nice Day at Red Rock

Introducing 'The SODS'

The short story competition was open to all first time writers, with fifty bucks being the prize for the best short story written. Abe couldn't wait to tell his pa about the story he had written and was going to submit.

"Pa, I want you to be the first to hear a story I've gone an' writ for a writer's competition to win me fifty bucks," Abe excitedly told his pa.

"Well, what's this story all about Abe?" asked his pa.

"Well sir, it's about this bunch of aliens from outer space called SODS, who come here looking for a place to call their own."

"Trinity?"

"It don't really matter which place pa, 'cause they ain't all here at the same time."

"They ain't?"

"No sir, some of 'em are still on board the Mother Ship, kinda just waiting, if you know what I mean?"

"Well patience is a virtue, that's what granny always used to say."

"Unless they charge by the hour, right pa?"

"You got that right."

Abe gave a disoriented look, having lost track just where he was at, in his story telling.

"Darned, if I ain't plum forgot where I was at."

It was pa to the rescue.

"Something about aliens?" his pa hinted.

It worked and Abe was back on track.

"That's right pa, and one of 'em's right here, mixing and chatting with folk who don't even know he's an alien."

"Ain't no shame in being an alien, been called one myself."

"How come pa?"

Abe's pa recollected an incident back in Red Rock, which he was happy to tell Abe about.

"Well, it happened one time back in Red Rock, when the buggy broke down. This policeman come on up to me and says, 'You're in a no parking zone. If, you don't move that heap, I'll have it towed.' Well now, gas being the price what it is an' all, I was real taken by his offer of help and says to him, 'That's real kind of you friend, let me give you my address so's you know where to take it.' Well, there come on over him, a change so sudden I could tell he was real offended. 'It ain't going to no address, it's going to the compound where it'll be kept under lock and key,' he says. Well, I ain't one to look a gift horse in the mouth and I sure didn't want to hurt his feelings none, but I told him straight. 'There ain't no need for that, it's safe enough at home,' and that's when he says to me, 'What are you, some kind of alien'?"

A similarity in his pa's tale with one in his own story, took Abe by surprise.

"If that ain't the strangest thing pa, 'cause there's even a policeman in my story, real friendly with the alien, and a fella without a job just like you, who takes a shine to him."

Abe's pa began to think that Abe might be in with a chance.

"Sound's to me as though you got every chance of winning that there fifty bucks, with this short story of yours. What's it called?"

"It's called The SODS, pa."

Abe's pa was suitably impressed.

"Well now, that's a real fancy title, I don't mind saying. How d'ya manage to think of that?"

"Heck, I didn't think of it pa, the author winston bradshaw did. All I gone done was to copy his book."

'The SODS'

A short story from the pen of winston bradshaw...*not Abe*

In loving memory of Auntie Chris
my world is a smaller place without you

Nice Day at Red Rock

Nice Day at Red Rock *written 2010*
First Published in Sweden by WBH Publishing 2011

Copyright © winston bradshaw 2011

The moral right of the author has been asserted.

Cover design winston bradshaw
Published by WBH Publishing
Bergsgatan 4A
771 34 Ludvika
Sweden
www.wbhpublishing.com

ISBN 978 91 978090 1 6

Printed and bound in the UK by Lightning Source,
Milton Keynes, England

Nice Day at Red Rock

winston bradshaw

WBH Publishing

"Our 'war on terror' begins with al Qaeda, but it does not end there..."
President George W Bush

It was another fine day that had Ike as usual sitting on the steps of the porch at the front of the house, a dilapidated old building dating back to the days of the civil war. Browsing the pages of an old newspaper, Ike stopped reading and looked up at the arrival of his son Abe in a less than desirable looking automobile, which they affectionately called General Lee after the confederate soldier of the same name.

Abe got out of the car and ambled on over to where his pa sat.

"Pa, where's Afghanistan?" Abe wanted to know.

Ike gave a thoughtful look which told Abe his pa's geography didn't stretch that far.

"Afghanistan? I don't rightly know. Why d'ya ask?"

"Well, there was this fella in uniform in

1

Herbie's store, telling Herbie he'd just come back from there..."

"You don't say."

"...and what's more, he told Herbie that him and the boys had been searching for this fella called Osama who's worth ten million bucks dead or alive."

"Well now, it don't seem to me that a fella would have much use for ten million bucks if he's dead, but it do show that if a fella comes into money they'll do anything it takes to find him. 'Course, that ain't always the case. When Truman passed on all Flora got was a letter telling her the stamp on it cost more than he'd left her."

At that moment Ike's sister Flora come on out of the house and onto the porch. Beaming a smile she looked at Abe.

"Well, did you win the short story competition?" she asked, with an air of optimism.

Hearing this jogged Ike's memory, who suddenly remembered that his boy Abe had written a short story, albeit not his own but the work of author winston bradshaw, entering it into a competition which offered fifty bucks prize money for the best short story written.

"A fine piece of writing if, ever there was, with a right fancy title. What was it called, 'The SODS'?"

"That's right pa. Fact is they ain't announced

the winner yet, but Miss. Scott, one of the judges let loose the beans by taking me to one side and confiding in me."

Ike was mildly surprised to hear this.

"She did, how come?"

"She called me a..."

Ike and Flora waited anxiously to hear the rest as Abe fumbled in his back pocket for a piece of scrap paper before reading what was written on it.

"Plagiarist...yes sir, that's what she called me alright, a plagiarist."

Wide eyed and with a smile to match Abe gave the look of a sure winner.

"I guess that means I've won, right pa?" said Abe proud as punch.

Ike scratched his chin.

"It sure do seem that way don't it," he agreed, clueless as to what plagiarist meant.

Flora was quick to concur.

"Sounds to me like we got ourselves another Mark Twain in the family," she enthused as Abe savored the moment.

Later that day a visitor called hoping to see Ike. Recognizing the visitor's car Abe went up and cheerfully greeted the man behind the wheel.

"Howdy Mr. Boswell."

"Please, Andrew," insisted Boswell, preferring to be on first name terms with his neighbors.

Abe immediately sought to correct what he thought to be an error on Boswell's part.

"Heck, you must have me confused with someone else Mr. Boswell, 'cause my name's Abe."

Boswell gave a wry grin.

"Yes, I know it is. Tell me Abe, is your pa home?"

"No sir, he's taken General Lee on over to Herbie's Store, but my guess is, it won't be long before he's back if, you wanna wait."

Boswell was more than impressed to hear that Ike was in the company of a General and was thereby in no hurry to leave, keen to make his acquaintance with General Lee.

"Well now, I'm in no hurry and I do need to speak with your pa, so why don't I just wait a while," said Boswell, who then got out of the car.

"Mr. Boswell, do you know where's Afghanistan?"

"Can't say that I do. Has General Lee been there?"

"No sir, General Lee ain't been no further than Chattanooga."

Boswell gave a puzzled look.

"Is there something wrong with the General?"

Abe cast a thought to the family automobile.

"I don't think so, apart from smokin' a little

too much, but that don't bother us none."

Boswell gave a weak smile unsure just what to make of what he had heard, as Abe spotted his pa at the wheel of General Lee approaching the house. On seeing Boswell, Ike warmly greeted his neighbor.

"Howdy Mr. Boswell, what brings you on over here?"

Boswell was surprised at seeing Ike alone.

"Haven't we forgotten something Mr. Broussard?" he asked Ike, giving a subtle hint at the whereabouts of General Lee.

Ike gave it a moment's thought then shook his head.

"I don't think so," he replied, somewhat puzzled.

"Well, where's General Lee?" enquired Boswell.

"General Lee's right here," said Ike, patting the car's bonnet whilst at the same time relieved that he had not forgotten anything.

Boswell gave an embarrassed smile.

"Are you feeling alright Mr. Boswell?" asked Ike.

"Might I have a word Mr. Broussard?" requested Boswell, brushing off his embarrassment.

"Surely Mr. Boswell. Why don't you come on up to the house and take a glass of lemonade," invited Ike.

Boswell sat facing Ike across the kitchen table, whilst Abe and Flora stood just a few feet away by the hot stove.

"Mr. Broussard, I wonder if I might impose upon you for a small favor?"

"Well now Mr. Boswell, that's what friends are for ain't it?"

"Yes, quite..."

Boswell hesitated a moment before continuing.

"...it's Charlene."

"Charlene?"

"My daughter Charlene. Oh, it's probably nothing, but try telling that to Mrs. Boswell."

"Is there some kind of problem Mr. Boswell?"

"The fact is, Charlene's been late coming home from school recently and it's got her mother just a little bit worried."

"Well, where d'ya suppose she goes?"

"Quite frankly I don't know which is why I've come to see you."

"Well, er, how can I help?"

"Her mother and I think it's possible that Charlene may have met someone through an internet chat room and is seeing that person after school."

"You mean a fella?"

"Precisely."

With pursed lips Ike expressed a thoughtful look and gave a nod as if, to indicate his clear understanding of Boswell's problem.

"I think I'm beginning to see your problem Mr. Boswell."

Boswell gave a relieved smile.

"I knew I could rely on you to understand Mr. Broussard."

"You want someone to act as a chaperone when they're together, so's they don't get up to any hanky panky, is that it?"

Boswell's smile disappeared, replaced with a straight face.

"Not exactly, I was thinking it would be more helpful if her mother and I knew just who it was Charlene was meeting after school."

"Well now, if that's all it is, why don't you give me the address of this chat room and I'll go there myself and see who it is," offered Ike.

"I'm afraid it's not quite that simple Mr. Broussard, but I would like to make an alternative suggestion, if I may?"

"Shoot."

Boswell threw a glance in Abe's direction.

"Well, how about if young Abe here was to follow Charlene after school to see who she meets? I'm sure once we know who it is, that'd put Mrs. Boswell's mind at rest."

"Well now, that don't sound like a bad idea to me," agreed Ike.

Abe was excited at the prospect of tailing Charlene.

"Heck, if I put on my moose head, she won't

even know it's me!" he cried.

"Mr. Boswell sir, wouldn't it be a whole lot easier if you just ask Charlene who it is she's meeting?" asked Flora.

"Oh, believe you me we've tried, but all she says is 'my lips are sealed'."

"I wish mine had been when Truman proposed," sighed Flora.

Charlene's cell phone rang, so she took the call. It was gramps, phoning to confirm the day, date and time of their arrival at the airport, where Charlene would meet them.

"I've got everything arranged for mom and dad's 25th but I think dad's a little bit suspicious," Charlene told gramps.

"Well, he gets that from your grandma."

Charlene gave a light chuckle.

"I still can't believe that mom and dad will be celebrating twenty five years of being married this coming Friday."

"Heck, that's nothing. I've had to put up with your grandma for twice that long," gramps joked.

"After school on Wednesday, I plan to go back to the DeVille Hotel, now that you've spoken with the manager there gramps, to make sure everything's gonna be just as we planned for mom and dad's special day, and then on Thursday I'll be in Red Rock to meet you and grandma at the airport."

"There's more to you than meets the eye," said gramps proudly.

The following day Abe loitered around the school waiting for Charlene to come out. When she did he followed her, keeping what he thought to be a safe distance between them, so as not to be spotted by her.

Barely had five minutes passed when she looked back. Quickly, Abe dropped to his feet and pretended to be tying his shoe laces. When he looked up Charlene was standing over him.

"Abe Broussard, are you following me?" she asked.

Abe struggled to think of an answer, saying the first thing which came into his head.

"My lips are sealed."

Charlene grinned.

"You've just given the game away."

With that said, Charlene turned and walked off leaving Abe with a conundrum and a blank look on his face. Getting onto his feet Abe ran after Charlene anxious that she should not click on to what he was up to.

"Fancy us bumping into each other like that," said Abe grinning like a Cheshire cat.

"Where are you going Abe?" Charlene coolly asked.

Abe's face lit up like a Christmas tree. The answer to where Charlene was going was now in his grasp.

"Well, where are you going?" responded Abe, throwing the question back at her.

"I asked first," said Charlene.

The lights went out as Abe yet again struggled to think of an answer.

That evening had Abe wondering how he would be able to follow Charlene the next day without being recognized. Fresh out of ideas he asked his pa and Flora for some.

"Seems to me, there's only one way a fella can avoid being recognized and that's, if he was to disguise himself. Kinda like one of them actors in the theatre, if you know what I mean," suggested Ike.

"If you ask me, all you need is a funny little moustache like that German fella during the war. That outta do it," added Flora.

Ike cast a thought to what Flora had said.

"Kinda makes you wonder don't it? Charlie Chaplin a German."

Flora was taken aback.

"I ain't meaning him," she made clear.

"Well, I dunno who you both talking about, but I know one thing for sure, it's got me all excited. Heck, I can't wait to see what I look like with a moustache," said Abe, before rushing off to get a paintbrush, scissors and some tape, the quintessential items he felt were needed to do the job.

Later on that evening whilst watching

television, Abe was struck at the sight of a Muslim woman dressed in a full length black veil and wearing a niqab, a piece of cloth which covered the woman's face from the eyes down. There was no doubt in Abe's mind that, the niqab was the perfect way to hide a person's face. Immediately he set about making a home made niqab, improvising as he did with a worn t-cloth and some rubber bands.

When he had finished Abe put on the face mask for all to see. At first Ike and Flora were lost for words, unsure just what to make of the mask. It wasn't long before Abe found out.

"Kinda striking, ain't it?" said Ike, scratching his cheek.

Hearing this put a smile on Abe's face, the outline of which could be seen through the mask.

"Some folk don't just got the mask. I've seen 'em on television covered all over from head to toe, as if they tryin' to hide from someone," said Abe excitedly.

"Is that a fact," acknowledged Ike.

Flora gave a mock laugh.

"Ain't no way a fella can hide wearing that getup. I see 'em once down Mississippi dressed like that, in white robes and wearing them funny hats. Tallest ice cream cones I ever did see. Bound to get you spotted."

Flora's remarks left Abe puzzled and brought the conversation to an end.

Late afternoon the following day, Officers O'Reilly and Klein sat in their patrol car munching on a burger.

"So, what did you do before you joined the Police?" O'Reilly asked the rookie Klein.

"Oh, well you know, I was with the Army in Iraq. That sort of thing."

"Iraq eh? I bet you had to do things out there you didn't like?"

Klein nodded.

"All the time. It was called 'going on patrol'."

"What about the people, were they friendly?"

"The people? You mean the Iraqis?"

"Yeah."

Klein shrugged.

"Oh, well you know, those who didn't shoot at us, I guess. Frankly, it's not the sort of place for a nice young Jewish boy like me. I wish I'd stayed home and gone into pawnbroking."

"An honorable profession sure enough but not quite the same as serving your country, and not forgetting them weapons of mass destruction."

"Oh, well you know, I wasn't actually there myself on the opening night in Baghdad, but I did catch the show on television. Shock an' awe, and all that stuff right?"

O'Reilly gave a puzzled look at Klein realizing that there had been something lost in translation. Iraq was suddenly forgotten as their attention was drawn to the other side of the road, where a young woman was seemingly being stalked by a man wearing a face mask.

"Well, would you look at that. If that ain't the strangest looking mask I ever did see," remarked O'Reilly, his attention firmly focused on the masked man.

Klein was similarly struck at the sight of the masked man.

"Well now, if I was a gambling man, which I'm not. That is, not unless you count the lottery, I'd lay odds on, that fella's trying to hide..."

O'Reilly's eyes widened, as he cut in on the rookie.

"Darn, we've just been spotted. He just looked over at us."

O'Reilly sunk down into his seat as the rookie Klein continued on rambling.

"...'course, on the other hand, he may not be trying to hide. Maybe he's got hmm... you know, a dermatological problem. I once had a small rash on my face which I always kept covered with a band-aid so's folk wouldn't see. I mean, what girls gonna want to kiss a fella, if she thinks he's got something contagious, right?" said Klein.

Klein got O'Reilly's attention.

"Well now, I dare say you're right, but as an experienced Police Officer, I gotta say the only people I know who a wear face mask during the day, are bank robbers."

"Oh, well you know, I've seen plenty of women in Iraq wearing face masks. Fact is, Arab women do. It's part of their culture."

O'Reilly was quick to make known his disapproval of this.

"You don't say. Well frankly I don't agree with women robbing banks."

With something lost in translation, this time on the part of O'Reilly, Klein tried to explain.

"Oh, well you know, you're absolutely right of course. Who does, right? But you see, it's not that kind of mask. It's er..."

Klein paused.

"...Oh, what the heck, do you suppose we outta go check him out?"

"That sounds like a good idea to me. Why don't you go check him out, whilst I finish off my burger?" suggested O'Reilly.

Klein wasn't happy with this.

"Me? You want me to go on my own? Suppose the fella turns out to be another Jeffrey Dahmer, how you gonna explain that down at the station?"

O'Reilly took a bite from his unfinished burger and Klein took the hint.

"OK then, well you know, if you're sure you don't wanna help, I suppose I could always...Oh, what the heck, here goes."

Within a couple of minutes Officer Klein stood confronting the masked man.

"Say, er, what is that you got on your face? Is that some sort of mask? Only it looks a bit like a... Is it a t-cloth? Is that what it is? Well, you know, if you got some kinda dermatological problem that's fine with me, only it's best you tell me straight 'cause you know... Well, between you and me, I've been there."

"My lips are sealed," said the masked man.

Klein gave a shrug.

"Oh, well you know, that's fine with me, but if you can just let me have your name, so's I know who I'm talking to and tell me why your wearing the er..."

Klein gestured with his hand intimating the mask.

"Why, this here's my disguise so's the person I'm following don't know it's me who's following 'em," said the masked man cheerfully.

Klein's eyes widened on hearing this.

"Oh, so what then? Does that mean the person you're following knows you?"

The masked man shook his head.

"No sir, not with my disguise on, she don't," he said as cheerful as ever.

Not exactly the answer that he expected, Klein mulled it over for a second or two.

"Oh, ok. Well you know, that's a straight enough answer and I appreciate that. Er, look, I tell you what, why don't you just give me a name?"

"Well, if I do that, you promise not to tell her it was me who told you."

It was another unexpected answer which had Klein mulling it over. They were joined by O'Reilly who took one look at the masked man and instantly knew who it was.

"Is that you Abe, hiding behind that mask?" asked O'Reilly.

"My lips are sealed," came the reply.

"Well then, how about you give us a nod, that'd be right fine by me."

Abe duly obliged with a decisive nod of the head. Satisfied, that the identity of the masked man had been established, O'Reilly took Klein to one side.

"I give Abe here, a parking ticket not so long ago. Strangest thing is, he's real happy with it. Shakes my hand and says, 'Are you sure you don't wanna give this to someone more deserving? 'cause I got me five of 'em already.' Well, I told him. I said, 'if you park here young fella, that's what you gonna get.' Abe says to me, 'This ain't the only place. I was given one by a real nice fella, just like you, outside city hall, who even promised to put a clamp on General Lee, if I was still there when he got back.' 'Now, why do you suppose that is?' I asked him, and Abe says, 'I guess so's no one will steal him, right?'..."

O'Reilly paused.

"...Take my advice. Let this one go."

Free to go, Abe continued on his way, but with the trail gone cold and with no sign of Charlene in sight, he decided to call it a day. As he turned the corner, Abe glimpsed the back of someone whom he thought to be Charlene entering the DeVille Hotel. Without a second thought he made his way over to the hotel and went in.

No sooner had Abe stepped foot inside the hotel lobby, when he was pounced upon by the Manager.

"Can I help you sir?" asked the Manager in a snooty voice.

Abe glanced around the lobby in the hope of spotting Charlene.

"I'm looking for a woman," replied Abe.

This caused a few raised eyebrows from those within hearing distance, which had the Manager give a weak smile at them with embarrassment.

"Well, I'm afraid you won't find one here. This is a respectable hotel," the Manager told Abe.

"You mean this hotel's just for men?"

"No, of course not. Now, you said something about a woman. Do I take it that you're here with someone?" probed the Manager.

"Well, I come with General Lee, but I left him in the car park."

Hearing such an important sounding name put a smile on the Manager's face.

"General Lee, you say? A most illustrious sounding name, if I say so myself. Had I known you were coming to the DeVille, the General could've parked out front, free of charge."

Abe beamed a smile that was clearly visible behind the mask.

"Heck, General Lee can park any place free of charge, 'cause I got me a parking ticket."

It wasn't just that Abe made no sense but the fact that he was sincere when he spoke, which baffled the Manager.

Ike and Flora listened as Abe made known to them his encounter that day with both the Police and the Manager of the DeVille Hotel.

"Why d'ya suppose, that policeman fella who recognized Abe, let the boy go Ike?" asked Flora.

"Stands to reason, don't it? He's the same one who took a shine to General Lee and gave Abe here, a parking ticket," replied Ike.

There was no doubt in Abe's mind that his pa was right.

"I reckon you're right there pa, although I get me the feeling they don't want folk to have more than one parking ticket."

"Is that right?"

"Yes sir, 'cause after he told me to 'run along there,' he said, 'and try not to collect any more of them parking tickets'."

Ike rubbed his chin as if to give it some thought.

"Well, now you got so many, maybe you should've offered to give one to the Manager of the DeVille. Reckon, he would've appreciated that," said Ike.

"I did that pa, and he come on over all funny and says to me, 'Do I look to you the kinda person who's gonna pay for someone's parking ticket?' so, I told him, it's free, but even that didn't cheer him up none."

Ike rubbed his chin again.

"Hmm, I guess there's just no pleasing some folk."

Abe carried on.

"So anyhow pa, then he asks me to take off my mask. So, I told him, 'I can't, 'cause if I do that, the person I'm following will recognize me.' 'Who's that?' he asked, so I told him, 'My lips are sealed.' So then, he asks me, 'Is it Elizabeth Taylor?' and I says, 'No sir, it's Charlene Boswell.' 'Well now, let me check which room she's in,' he says, and went off to talk with some woman standing behind a desk..."

Ike cut in.

"I guess, to save you some time."

"Right considerate, if you ask me," added Flora.

Abe continued on.

"...well anyhow, when he comes back, he

19

says, 'She ain't in any room.' So then, I gets me thinking, and says, 'I guess she sneaked out the back door.' 'Our visitors come and go by the front door, but in your case I'm gonna make an exception,' he says to me in a loud voice, so's other folk can hear. Well, I knew then, that I was being treated kinda special and he wanted them other folk to know it."

Ike exchanged a smile with Flora.

"Sounds to me, as though you made a real impression on the fella, for him to make an exception like that," said Ike.

Hearing this brought back fond memories for Flora.

"Reminds me of my first date with Truman, when he took me for a meal at Hank's Burger Bar. 'I ain't gonna let you pay for the meal...' I told him, '...we'll split the bill and go halves.' He give me that saucy smile of his and says, 'When I take a fine young lady out for a meal, I always pay, but in your case sweet lady, I'll make an exception'."

Flora paused and gave a smile as she fondly remembered the occasion.

"He sure knew how to treat a woman," she sighed.

Her reminiscing was broken by Abe.

"Who's Elizabeth Taylor?" he asked.

It was Thursday, and school was out. For Abe, trying hard not to be spotted by Charlene, on a crowded bus going to the airport, brought some suspicious looks from his fellow passengers.

"Have you got swine flu?" asked the elderly Negro, sitting next to him on the bus.

"No sir, I don't got it," replied Abe.

"Well then, why are you wearing a mask?"

"I'm wearing this mask so's not to be spotted, like them folk done, down in Mississippi."

"What folk might they be?"

"The one's with the ice cream cones."

The elderly Negro shook his head with dismay.

"This country ain't never gonna change," he muttered, before turning away and gazing out of the window.

When the bus arrived at the airport, Abe followed Charlene into the terminal. Still wearing his home-made mask, he was conspicuous as a black face would be at a gathering of the Ku Klux Klan, drawing attention to himself not only from passing travelers but also airport security.

At Iranian Airways check-in desk, Abe swiftly ducked to avoid being spotted by Charlene, when she glanced back over her shoulder.

When he got to his feet a few moments later, Abe came face to face with an Arab woman dressed in a full length black veil and wearing a niqab, who together with her husband was checking in for a flight. Abe was mega impressed with her niqab and using sign language offered to do a swap with the woman for his own home-made one. Sadly, it was not to be as Abe continued on with his tail of Charlene, once more having to duck at a Hertz Car Rental desk, to avoid detection by her.

Whilst still in a crouching position, Abe felt a tap on his shoulder. Looking up he saw two men in uniform standing over him. They were airport security.

"Would you mind getting up from that desk," said one of the men.

"I sure will, just as soon as I know the coast is clear," responded Abe.

"Well, I'm afraid I can't wait that long, so if you don't mind," insisted the man.

Abe got to his feet.

"We've been watching you, and I'd like you to come with us," the man told Abe.

"Heck, I'd sure like to oblige, but I'm kinda busy just now. Could you maybe, ask someone else?" Abe cheerfully suggested.

With hands on hips the man gave Abe a 'no nonsense' look.

"Well now, I don't think you understand. This is not a request," said the man.

"Does that mean I don't have to go?" asked Abe.

The two security men exchanged a puzzled glance with one another before the one doing the talking, took hold of Abe's arm.

"Come with us," he said, leading the way.

"OK, but I can't stay long," Abe let it be known.

At a cordoned off area of the terminal the man released Abe's arm.

"Are you carrying any weapons or sharp instruments on you?" he asked Abe.

"Sharp instruments?"

"Like scissors for example," clarified the man.

Abe shook his head.

"No sir, but I can go fetch a pair, if you promise to give 'em back," offered Abe.

"We don't want no scissors. We just wanna know, if you got any on you?"

The man quickly retracted his words.

"Let me rephrase that. If you got any scissors on you, we want 'em."

Abe expressed a puzzled look.

"I'm confused," he said.

With tongue-in cheek the man thought a moment.

"Perhaps it's best if we just pat you down but first, I'm gonna have to ask you to take off the mask."

The man sensed that Abe was reluctant to do this and felt that some reassurance was necessary.

"You don't need to be shy, there's no one here only us and we've seen everything, ain't that right Bob?" said the man, turning to his colleague.

Bob, who had been silent up until this moment, now spoke.

"That's right Dick, there ain't nothing we ain't seen."

Hearing this and knowing that Charlene wasn't around put Abe at his ease, and so he took off the mask. Both men fell silent at the sight now confronting them, and for a moment or so were completely lost for words.

"Is that for real?" asked Bob, putting a hand to his mouth.

Abe took Bob's comment as nothing short of praise.

"Made it myself," said Abe proudly, as he gently stroked the paint brush hairs under his nose, that were held together with tape.

Bob's colleague Dick cleared his throat, before speaking.

"Would you mind removing the...er, moustache as well," he requested.

Having removed the home-made niqab and moustache, a further request was then made for Abe to raise his arms and spread his feet, so that a body search could be carried out on him. Since Abe had never undergone a body search before and failed to grasp what he was supposed to do, resulted in Bob having to demonstrate for Abe, the posture he was required to adopt.

After the body search, which revealed

nothing other than an old parking ticket and some sweet wrappings, Abe was briefly quizzed by Dick.

"Would you mind telling me your name? Just for the record, that is," asked Dick, as he got ready to write it down.

Abe was only too happy to oblige.

"My name's Abe."

"OK, and er, how do you spell that?"

"A.B.E."

Dick wrote it down.

"You got a last name?"

"Yes sir."

"Do you mind telling me what it is?"

"No sir."

Dick waited until his patience ran out.

"Well, what is it?"

"Broussard."

"Broussard," repeated Dick, whilst jotting it down.

"Well now Abe, it don't seem to me, to be a sensible thing to be wearing a mask inside an airport terminal. So, can you tell me why you was wearing one?"

Abe beamed a smile.

"Heck, I ain't the only one wearing a mask here, I seen other folk wearing 'em too."

Dick was surprised to learn that there were other masked folk in the terminal who had gone undetected by airport security.

"What other folk?" Dick wanted to know.

"The same folk that was on television."

"On television?" repeated Dick.

"Yes sir, only they got a much better mask than me."

"Well now, I'm sure if there was anyone wearing a mask inside this terminal we'd have spotted them, just like we did you."

"If you want, I can go tell them that you're looking for 'em."

"Well never mind them, just tell us why you're wearing a mask. Have you got swine flu?"

"No sir, I don't got it, but it sure seem to me, a lotta folk trying to get their hands on it, 'cause a fella on the bus asked me the same thing."

Dick gave a frustrated sigh.

"Why do I get this feeling that I'm talking to myself?" he voiced.

Abe smiled.

"Heck, I wouldn't let that bother you none. I hear folk say that all the time."

Dick tried once more to find out why Abe was wearing a mask.

"Well now Abe, since you don't got swine flu, it kinda figures to me you must've been wearing a mask for some other reason, ain't that right?"

"Yes sir, so's I ain't spotted."

Dick gave a satisfied smile.

"Ah, ha, I guess we got that right. So then,

what was the next part of the plan? Try sneaking onto a plane, maybe?"

Still smiling, Abe shook his head.

"No sir, I'm going back on the bus," said Abe.

Dick was left with a dead pan expression on his face and back where he started.

Spotting Harland Mitchell ex-FBI, head of airport security and an expert on counter terrorism, Dick went off to have a word in his ear, leaving Abe in the company of Bob.

"Well now Abe, I couldn't help notice you got a parking ticket, which kinda means you got yourself a car, don't it? So, how come you going back on the bus?" asked Bob more than a little curious.

"Heck, that parking ticket ain't mine, it belong to General Lee," replied Abe.

"General Lee?"

"If you like, I can go fetch General Lee and bring him on over for you to see?" offered Abe, with some enthusiasm.

With pursed lips, Bob shook his head.

"No, no, no, that won't be necessary. But, it might be helpful, if you could tell me where we can find General Lee."

"Well, when I get back into town, General Lee gonna take me home."

"Oh, so then, General Lee's family, is that right?"

"He sure is," said Abe proudly.

"I guess you must sleep soundly at night knowing there's a General in the house?"

Abe gave a chuckle which left Bob wondering.

"General Lee don't sleep in the house, we leave him outside."

"Outside? Seems a bit harsh, don't it?"

"No sir, 'cause if it gets too cold, pa just give him some anti-freeze."

Bob gave an embarrassed cough and swiftly changed direction. Picking up a sheet of paper from off a table, he handed it to Abe.

"Here's a list of places on the axis of evil. Have you visited any of 'em in the last twelve months?"

"I been to Chattanooga," said Abe, not bothering to look at the list.

Bob took back the paper.

"Do you know where's Afghanistan?" asked Abe.

"Not so's I'd know it on a map. Why? Are you planning on visiting friends there?"

"No sir, but a fella come into Herbie's store saying, him and the boys was there, looking for someone called Osama, who's worth ten million bucks dead or alive."

Bob set the record straight.

"You must be talking about Osama bin laden. He ain't worth ten million bucks, he's worth twenty five million bucks, and everyone out there's looking for him. I only wish it was me, who could find him."

"Reckon he'd be right pleased to see you. Might even give you a reward for finding him?" said Abe.

Bob forced a smile, unsure just what to make of Abe.

A couple of minutes later Dick returned and took Bob to one side.

"I've just had a word with Harland, him being an expert an' all. He's agreed to have a chat with this young fella, to see what he can make of him," said Dick in a low voice.

Bob looked apprehensive.

"I don't think that's a good idea," he said.

Dick was adamant.

"Well, it's too late now, I've already asked, so, let's wheel him in."

Abe was escorted to the office of Harland Mitchell, where he sat facing the man himself, across the great divide, a mahogany desk. There, in silence they sat, for what seemed to Abe an eternity, as Mitchell studied Abe's face as if it were the face of Carlos the Jackal. When Mitchell spoke, it was the voice of experience.

"I can spot a terrorist at five hundred yards. Are you a terrorist, Abe?" asked Mitchell, as if unsure.

Abe smiled.

"Heck, I wouldn't know about that, but it sure sounds to me as if, you got better eyesight than a bald eagle."

Mitchell gave a half-hearted smile as he pondered his next move. It was just a matter of seconds.

"Why don't we cut to the chase and try to establish just what it is you're doing here," he suggested to Abe.

"Are you going some place? Flying off somewhere, maybe?"

Still smiling, Abe shook his head.

"No sir."

"Well then, are you here to meet someone?"

Again, Abe shook his head.

"No sir."

"Well, now you see Abe, that's my dilemma. You've just about eliminated the only two good reasons you got for you being at the airport. So, why are you here?"

"Heck I dunno, but I'm sure having fun."

"Well, I'm glad someone's having a good time. Now, perhaps you wouldn't mind telling me if, you came here with anyone?"

"I told 'em I couldn't be staying long but, I guess they didn't wanna ask anyone else."

Mitchell was intrigued.

"Who's 'they?" he wanted to know.

"The two fellas I come here with."

"That's more like it..." said Mitchell, reaching for a pen.

"...now if you can just let me have their names."

"Well sir, one of 'em's called Bob and the other one's called Dick."

Any hope Mitchell had of exposing a terrorist plot instantly evaporated on hearing the two names, which were all too familiar to him.

"Now see here Abe, whatever it is you're doing here, we'll find out sooner or later 'cause you're dealing with experts. Fact is, without you even knowing it, we was profiling you the minute you entered the terminal."

Clearly surprised at this, Abe let it be known just how he felt about it.

"Well heck, I ain't never been profiled before, but I know one thing for sure, it don't hurt, 'cause I never felt a thing."

Mitchell took Abe's comment in his stride.

"Whilst I admire your sense of humor Abe, you gotta appreciate that our country's fighting the war on terror, and we have to deal firmly with anyone perceived to be a threat. Now, we know you speak Arabic, 'cause you was spotted communicating with an Arab woman at the Iran Air desk, and soon afterwards, you was caught at Hertz trying to avoid detection."

Mitchell paused, and with a glimmer of a smile, gave the look of one who already knew the answer to the question, he was about to ask. Whilst slowly nodding his head, as if to encourage Abe to give the answer he wanted, Mitchell let drop.

"Are you al-Qaeda?"

31

Abe's response was as usual both forthright and sincere.

"No sir I ain't, but if you show me what he looks like, I'll tell you if I've seen him."

With a dead pan look Mitchell took a moment to recover from the answer then forged on.

"If, you ain't no terrorist, then how come you was seen communicating to an Arab woman at Iran Air, after which, you then tried to evade detection?"

"I ain't sure I know what you mean."

Mitchell could see from the look on Abe's face that he needed a gentle reminder. Grabbing a piece of paper from off his desk Mitchell covered over his nose and mouth with it.

"The woman wearing a burkha? Face covered?"

Abe suddenly remembered.

"I'd recognize that face anywhere."

Mitchell let drop the paper.

"So, then you do know her?"

"She was on the television."

"You saw her on television? But, how can you be sure it's the same person? She was covered head to toe and wearing a burkha."

"Just like on television."

Mitchell gave a shrug.

"Well, I suppose it's possible, but if I was a betting man, I wouldn't put money on it."

"Did you say we was fighting the war on terror?" asked Abe.

"That's right," replied Mitchell, wondering what was coming next.

"Well, who are we fighting?"

"That rather depends whose side you're on, wouldn't you say?"

"Well, whose side are you on?" Abe wanted to know.

Mitchell began to feel the strain.

"Like I told you, our country's fighting the war on terror. The common enemy is al-Qaeda, as I'm sure you already know."

What Abe hadn't known before, he did now.

"You mean we're fighting just one fella? Well heck, what's he gone done?"

"Don't you watch television?" asked Mitchell, trying to keep his cool.

"Only when the Simpson's are on," replied Abe.

"Look, just tell me why you was wearing a mask inside the terminal then maybe we can wrap this whole thing up."

"My lips are sealed," said Abe.

"Well, maybe you can unseal 'em for just one minute. How would that be?"

Abe gave it some thought and relented.

"My mask is a disguise, so's the person I'm following don't know it's me who's following 'em."

"Oh, I see, and who might that be Abe?"

Abe smiled.

"I guess you're thinking it's Elizabeth Taylor, right?"

Mitchell forced another smile.

"The thought had crossed my mind."

"Well, you'd be wrong. It's Charlene Boswell."

Unlike Elizabeth Taylor's name, Charlene Boswell's didn't ring any bells with Mitchell.

"Who's Charlene Boswell?" he asked Abe.

"Mr. Boswell's daughter," replied Abe.

"Well, who's Mr. Boswell?"

Abe gave a light chuckle.

"Well heck, even I know that. He's Charlene's pa."

"So, you're wearing a mask in this terminal, 'cause you're following Charlene Boswell, is that it?"

Abe nodded.

"Yes sir."

"And why are you following her?" asked Mitchell as he wrote down her name on a piece of paper.

"Well, I ain't found that out yet, but when I do, I gotta tell Mr. Boswell."

Realizing that he had come to a dead end again, Mitchell put down his pen.

"Well, be that as it may, you can't go around this terminal wearing a mask. Why, you might easily have been mistaken for a terrorist hijacker, or even worse a suicide bomber, in which case my men would've had no choice but to put you through one of our scanners."

Mitchell's high regard and admiration for the airport scanners soon became apparent, as he sank back in his chair and began pouring praise on them.

"Yes sir, state of the art technology are them scanners. Why, they can show a 3D image of a person's anatomy clearer than if they was opened up on a mortuary slab, which means, they can see through you even better than I can," he proudly boasted.

Abe was more than impressed.

"Gosh, I sure wish I had me one of them scanners. Could tell me what kinda candy I'm getting even before I unwrap it, 'case I don't like it, that is."

Mitchell straightened up, anxious now to be rid of Abe.

"Well now Abe, I've got some good news. You're free to go, just so long as you promise, not to put on the mask again until you've left the airport. Agreed?"

"But, if I don't have a mask on, I'll be spotted by Charlene."

Mitchell gave a shrug.

"Well, I'm sorry Abe, but that's the deal."

"I ain't the only one here wearing a mask."

Aware of just who Abe was referring to, Mitchell sought quickly to defend his decision.

"Well, I know that, but the woman at Iran Air

is a Muslim and an Arab. You ain't..."

Mitchell paused, noting Abe's glum look, before continuing.

"...It's part of their culture. Look, I don't make the rules, that's the way it is, right," he concluded.

Mitchell could see that Abe wasn't happy and so, made a concession.

"Well, how about if we let you keep the moustache?" he suggested.

Abe was appeased and it showed.

"I heard there's a German fella, got one just like me," said Abe.

Mitchell was indifferent.

"I can't imagine who, and I doubt his would attract the attention yours does."

Abe was inclined to agree.

"I reckon you're right, 'cause another fella called Charlie Chaplin got the same moustache as him."

Abe got Mitchell's attention.

"You're wearing an Adolf Hitler moustache? Is that what you're saying?" asked Mitchell.

Abe beamed his usual smile.

"Heck no, I got my own."

Mitchell gave up, and pushed a button on his desktop phone system. Then, talking on an open line, told the person at the other end to come into his office. It was Bob.

"Well now Abe, we've had ourselves a little chat, and it's for sure you ain't no terrorist or al-Qaeda, so, I don't think we need detain you any longer. Bob here will see you out."

"If you like, when I'm finished what I'm doing, I can come back and help you look for this fella al-Qaeda," offered Abe.

Mitchell raised a hand.

"No, that won't be necessary, but a word of advice Abe. Don't go wearing a mask inside an airport terminal. You was lucky it was Bob here and not an armed response unit, otherwise it might have escalated into something more serious. Someone might have got shot, if you catch my meaning?"

Abe gave his customary smile.

"I don't reckon so, 'cause I got me no gun. Besides, it wouldn't be right to go shooting at folk, right?"

Just before leaving the room, Abe took something out of his pocket.

"I sure had me a fine time here, and I'd like you to have this," he told Mitchell, handing him an old parking ticket.

Mitchell looked at the parking ticket then back at Abe, as if for some explanation.

"Don't worry, it's free..." Abe assured Mitchell. "...I got me five of 'em already."

With that said, Abe left the room escorted by Bob, leaving Mitchell staring at the parking ticket, totally baffled.

"He sure is a nice fella," said Abe referring to Mitchell.

Bob smiled.

"Harland reckons he can spot a terrorist at five hundred yards."

"Yes sir, I know, but his eyesight ain't as good as a scanner, right?"

Bob gave a light chuckle before bidding farewell to Abe.

As Abe walked past the shops in the terminal he could not help but notice an A-board on a stand outside one of them. The A-board promoted a newspaper with big headline wording intended to catch the eye of any passer by. 'THE SEARCH FOR OSAMA CONTINUES,' the wording screamed out and was accompanied by a dated picture of Osama bin laden emerging from his hideaway cave in the mountains of Afghanistan. Dressed in local clothing and wearing a turban, bin laden looked gaunt and poverty stricken.

As Abe stood there gazing at the picture of bin laden, he was joined by an old lady hauling a suitcase on wheels. With a look of disdain on her face, she cocked back her head at bin laden's picture.

"I sure hope they find him soon, 'cause if anyone deserves to get what's coming to 'em, he does," she sneered.

Abe couldn't agree more.

"I hope they find him too 'cause he sure look as if he could use the money."

Stumped at hearing this, the old lady gave a cursory glance at Abe, then despairing went on her way.